FIREFLY NIGHT

Carole Gerber

Illustrated by Marty Husted

Whispering Coyote
A Charlesbridge Imprint

To Mark, my alpha wolf
—C.G.

To John
—M.H.

Author's Note

During the early part of the nineteenth century, the Chippewa people, also called the Ojibwa, lived on plains west of the Great Lakes. Severe weather made farming difficult, so bands of families traveled together to fish, hunt, and gather wild plants. Each time they settled a new village, the Chippewa built dome-shaped wigwams framed with saplings and covered with mats made of natural materials. In warm weather, their children often slept outdoors in cradles just like the one in this story.

—Carole Gerber

Text copyright © 2000 by Carole Gerber
Illustrations copyright © 2000 by Marty Husted
All rights reserved, including the right of reproduction
in whole or in part in any form.

A **Whispering Coyote** Book
Published by Charlesbridge Publishing
85 Main Street
Watertown, MA 02472
(617) 926-0329
www.charlesbridge.com

Library of Congress Cataloging-in-Publication Data

ISBN 1-58089-051-2 (reinforced for library use)
ISBN 1-58089-066-0 (softcover)

Printed in China
(hc) 10 9 8 7 6 5 4 3 2 1
(sc) 10 9 8 7 6 5 4 3 2 1

Illustrations done in watercolors and color pencil on Arches cold press watercolor paper
Display type and text type set in Tiffany Demi Italic and 16-point Garamond
Separated and manufactured by Toppan Printing Co.
Book production by *The Kids at Our House*
Designed by *The Kids at Our House*

Wah-wah-taysee, little firefly,
Little, flitting, white-fire insect,
Little, dancing, white-fire creature,
Light me with your little candle,
Ere upon my bed I lay me,
Ere in sleep I close my eyelids.

The Song of Hiawatha
Henry Wadsworth Longfellow

Firefly, guide my way to sleep
in the forest, green and deep.
Shine your light above my head.
Lead me to my cradle bed.

Wah-wah-taysee, firefly;
name for you from Chippewa.

Flash your golden signal bright
as the evening turns to night.

Magic beetle, bring your glow
to the forest's nighttime show.
Light up the woods so I can see
all that hide, *Wah-wah-taysee*.

Show me the fox, the wolf, the hare.

Show me the grizzly's hidden lair.

Reveal the secrets of this night,
Wah-wah-taysee, with your light.

Illuminate the marshy bog.

Shine on the turtle, snake, and frog.

Flash your lantern; show to me
the muskrat's home, *Wah-wah-taysee.*

Show me the owl, the goose, the duck.

Light up the fawn, the doe, the buck.

With gentle steps, so quietly,
I'll follow you, *Wah-wah-taysee.*

And now I've reached my sleeping place.

Shine your sweet light upon my face.

Then fly into my dreams with me,